PARLOR
A
B
DINER
COACH
NUMBERS
E 1
E 2
E 3
CLUB-LOUNGE

TR

12-00 A.M.

CECIL BUNIONS
AND THE
MIDNIGHT TRAIN

Betty Paraskevas

ILLUSTRATED BY

Michael Paraskevas

Harcourt Brace & Company

SAN DIEGO   NEW YORK   LONDON

Library of Congress Cataloging-in-Publication Data

Paraskevas, Betty.
Cecil Bunions and the midnight train/Betty Paraskevas;
illustrated by Michael Paraskevas.
p.   cm.
Summary: A young boy has a dreamlike adventure on
the Midnight Super Train where he meets Cecil Bunions,
a private eye.
ISBN 0-15-292884-7
[1. Railroads—Trains—Fiction. 2. Adventure and
adventurers—Fiction. 3. Stories in rhyme.]
I. Paraskevas, Michael, 1961–   ill. II. Title.
PZ8.3.P162Ce   1996
[E]—dc20   95-30692

First edition
A B C D E

PRINTED IN SINGAPORE

The illustrations in this book were done in gouache on
bristol board.
The display type was set in Bovine Poster.
The text type was set in Esprit.
Color separations by Bright Arts, Ltd., Singapore
Printed and bound by Tien Wah Press, Singapore
This book was printed with soya-based inks on Leykam
recycled paper, which contains more than 20 percent
postconsumer waste and has a total recycled content of
at least 50 percent.
Production supervision by Warren Wallerstein and
Pascha Gerlinger
Designed by Michael Farmer

To Dr. Peter J. Raia,
the lovely Stavroula,
and Christopher,
and
to Jim and Lisa Mendelson,
Jenna, Bobby, and Scott

—B. P. and M. P.

2861

A COLD WIND touched my hand and stirred the pages as I read.
A shadow crossed the room. I saw a face beside my bed.
He seemed to be familiar, like a face that I had seen
Featured as a villain upon the silver screen.

The clock turned pale; with trembling hands, it pointed to the time.
Midnight was the hour, but the clock refused to chime.
The stranger took my hand and led me through the night.
I was standing on a platform, dazzled by the sight.

I saw the Midnight Super Train, sleek in classic black.
Light spilled from her windows. She was breathing on the track.
The conductor shouted, "All aboard!" The signal lights turned green.
"She'll take you to a better place, with no stops in between."

The stranger boosted me aboard as the train began to slide.
It was too late to jump off. I was doomed to take that ride.
All the passengers were talking. Through the windowpane,
I watched my city slip away and listened to the train.
She seemed to chant a message as she raced along the track:
NEVER COMING, NEVER COMING, NEVER COMING BACK.

Wasn't anybody listening? In an instant I could see
That no one heard the warning of that midnight train but me.
Everyone was talking and suddenly I found
The voices most disturbing. Their loud and hollow sound
Made it hard to hear the warning as she raced along the track—
NEVER COMING, NEVER COMING, NEVER COMING BACK.

I made my way to the dining car. An arrogant waiter said,
"We're only serving peanut butter sprayed on whole wheat bread."
"But I don't like that," I replied. He answered with a smile,
"You'll learn to love it, trust me, when you've been here for a while."

The crowd was in a festive mood. As the waiter turned away,
A man across the table winked and I heard him softly say,
"Allow me to introduce myself. My name is Cecil Bunions.
I'm a private eye and those who know me say I know my onions."

"I'm happy to know you, Mr. Bunions.
But what does it mean to know your onions?"
"It means I'm the best at what I do,
But as a private eye, I'm telling you,
I don't know how I got here. I must have been asleep.
That's the only way I could be led astray
with all the rest of these sheep."

"Mr. Bunions," I confided, "this is difficult to explain.
Do me a favor. Close your eyes and listen to the train."
He closed his eyes and listened as we raced along the track.
"EUREKA, LAD! I HEAR IT. . . SHE'S NEVER COMING, NEVER COMING,

   NEVER COMING BACK!"

We pressed our faces to the window.
The train was racing through the sky.
Far below us was a river. "I believe it's time to try
To wake up from this nightmare," Mr. Bunions said.
"I must find a way to get you safely back to bed."

We hurried to the engine. Mr. Bunions knocked.
When no one answered, he tried the door and found that it was locked.
He was silent for a moment and then I heard him say,
"Come on, lad. We have one chance, one chance to get away."

The passengers were sleeping as we scrambled to go back
And see if we could disconnect the last car on the track.
When we reached our destination, we found a herd of woolly sheep.
"EUREKA, LAD!" cried Bunions. "NOW I *KNOW* THAT I'M ASLEEP!"

He knelt near the opened door, struggled to loosen the bolt.
The train was moving faster. I felt a sudden jolt.
The cars were disconnected. That lady said good-bye,
Blasting her powerful whistle as she streaked across the sky.

We continued rolling backward till I heard Mr. Bunions shout,
"Look, lad, there's our city! Be careful getting out."
Woolly white sheep were smothering me as I tumbled out the door.
When I opened my eyes, I landed hard upon my bedroom floor.

Weeks went by and then one day, as I crossed the avenue,
I saw him again. Cecil Bunions. I didn't know what to do.
He gave no sign that he knew me, till just as he passed me by,
He tipped his hat and winked. I watched that private eye
Disappear into the crowd, leaving me to wonder:
WAS I AWAKE OR WAS I ASLEEP—OR WAS IT A SPELL I WAS UNDER?